The Game's a Foot

A Captain Finn Treasure Mystery

LIZ DODWELL

Mix Books, LLC

Liz Dodwell

The Game's a Foot: A Captain Finn Treasure Mystery
Copyright © 2015 by Liz Dodwell

www.lizdodwell.com

Print ISBN-13: 978-1-939860-20-0

Published by Mix Books, LLC

www.mix-booksonline.com

Table of Contents

One

Time Voyager swayed with the rhythm of the water as we lay at anchor on the Boneyard site in the Gulf of Mexico. On deck, Grace and Michael Bumbry had stripped off their dive gear and settled into a couple of chairs. They were happy, which meant Finn and I were happy.

The Bumbrys were occasional sponsors of our shipwreck treasure hunting expeditions. The quid pro quo for that was a share in potential finds, and the chance to come diving with us. Grace and Michael were active members of NABS, The National Association of Black Scuba Divers and were keen amateur historians of slavery. As such, they had opted for a week at the site where Finn believed we might find evidence of a slave ship.

We hadn't uncovered any major finds, but Michael did turn up a piece of pewter that Finn surmised was the handle of a spoon. That got everyone's adrenalin going because it told us we were likely on the right track. And from Finn's and my point of view, it also meant we could be assured of the Bumbry's continued support.

This was the family's last night. Oh, did I mention Joshua? He's their eleven year-old son; a quiet, serious boy, but smart as they come. He'd earned his Junior Open Waters Divers certification just a couple of months earlier, so had been underwater with his parents and had collected a whole mess of fossils. The Boneyard site gets its name because the area is replete with fossilized bones, teeth and shells. In his horde Joshua had megalodon teeth, – that's an extinct shark that grew to 60 feet, *Yikes!* – whale ear bones, rib bones and vertebrae. These were all from the Pleistocene epoch, dating back 12,000 to 2,500,000 years ago. And if you think I sound as if I know what I'm talking about, I actually haven't a clue. I'm just passing on the information I got from young Joshua.

So, back to the story. Finn was sort of holding court with treasure tales, though both Grace and Michael were giving him a run for his money. *No wonder Joshua was so quiet, he probably couldn't get a word in edgeways.* Finn was in the midst of describing the procedure a constipated pirate might have to endure back in the 1600 and 1700s. "They'd shoot anything from alcohol to tobacco or even gunpowder up there."

"That must have been pretty explosive," Michael grinned.

In turn his wife quipped, "Thank goodness those remedies have all been flushed down the drain."

Everyone groaned, including Jafet Quintana and Enos Donnell, who regularly crewed with us when we worked the Boneyard. They were all waiting for me to bring out the pre-dinner cocktails – except Joshua, of course. He was busy with his fossils.

I'd come up with a special creation to observe this final evening: a mix of toasted almond liqueur, dark rum, a little almond milk; shaken and served up with a dash of spicy Cayenne. In light of the conversation I decided right there and then I was going to name the drink a Clap of Thunder.

"Here we go!" I carried the cocktails out on a tray and handed them around. Grace was now showing Finn the video she'd been taking all week. She had funny clips of us talking pirate-speak, serious clips of how we set up a search grid, and lots of underwater scenes. I left them to it. On board my role was chief cook and bottle washer and I needed to get back in the galley and start prepping dinner.

Joshua was still examining his fossils.

"What are you going to do with them all?" I asked.

"Weeell. I need to finish identifying them all first. Like this one." He held up a large squarish fossil. "I think this might be a whale vertebra. And this one…" about the size of a fat finger, "could be a deer antler."

"How would that get out here?"

"I'm not sure." His frown created deep parentheses between his eyebrows. "It's a puzzle."

"One I'm sure you'll solve," I said, thinking how he sounded so much older than his years.

He nodded sagely before continuing, "Then I'll take them in to school to show the other kids."

I was about to respond when there was a shriek from the deck. I dashed out, thinking the worst, only to find everyone bunched around Grace with her video-cam. "Phill," she yelled excitedly at me, "we've found it, or at least we've found something. Come see."

I peered over her shoulder at the screen. "Finn says they could be elephant tusks."

It took me a few moments to focus in on what she was pointing at, then I saw it. The outline of four curved objects lying together like spoons in a drawer under a heavy layer of sediment.

"Don't get too excited yet," Finn cautioned. "They could be mammoth tusks, though that's unlikely with the way they're lying. Or it could be a trick of the ocean bed. And we need to figure out where they are first."

I raised questioning eyebrows.

"I don't know exactly where I was when I filmed this," Grace said. "According to the time stamp, it was on day three."

"Well, shi…." *Oops, I was supposed to be watching my language around Joshua.* "Well, surely that's not an insurmountable problem?" I was getting caught up in the excitement. This could be huge.

Someone tugged at my arm. I looked down to see my young friend. His eyes were wide and soundlessly he beckoned with a wave of his fingers for me to follow. At the side of the deck he pointed across the water. "There's something out there, Phill. See? That pink thing?"

I followed the line of his arm with my eyes. There *was* something; a piece of pink flotsam, though it was impossible to say at this distance what it was. My first inclination was to dismiss it, but then I looked at Joshua.

"What do you think it is?" he asked. *What the hell.* The grown-ups were having their excitement, why not let Joshua have his? At least for a few minutes.

"The current is bringing it towards us. You go and get the landing net; the telescoping one." He looked at me blankly. "The one that extends." With a brief nod of understanding, he dashed off and was soon back with the net. I let it out to its full 18 feet and we both stood, expectantly, as the object bobbed slowly closer.

Several minutes later I was stretching out trying to snag the flotsam. I still couldn't tell what it was and I just couldn't quite reach it either. If I didn't do something quickly it was going to bob right on by. I snatched some line, tied it round my waist and then to the gunwale rail. Allowing the line to hold some of my weight I was able to gain a few extra inches; enough to tease the object into the net. Then I steadily pulled it in.

It was just a sneaker. A neon pink, child's size air sneaker. Those things will float forever.

"I'm sorry, buddy." I held the net out to him. He didn't look nearly as disappointed as me, but picked the shoe up and studied it intently. *Funny kid. Fossils one minute, yucky sneakers the next.* I turned away to get back to my culinary duties.

"Phill."

I swung back to face him. "Yeah?"

"There's a foot in it."

Two

Detective Dixie Tanner was one fine looking woman. We'd met her a while back when we got involved in a murder of a one-armed man in Sarasota. She and Finn had become close, if you know what I mean. In her fifties, she wore spiked heels and strutted her stuff as well as any runway model. She'd also changed her hair color to a coppery blonde that looked really good on her. Self-consciously I tried to fluff up my short sun-bleached locks as I listened to her.

"The odds are heavily against us ever finding out who the shoe belonged to. Any flesh has long gone; there was just bone held together by a sock. Assuming the child drowned, the M.E. tells me it's likely the foot broke free from the body as it decomposed. The buoyancy from the air in the shoe would allow it to float away."

"How long would it take before the ankle broke? Maybe we can figure out where the body first entered the water." For some reason I felt the little girl – with a pink shoe it must surely be a girl – deserved more than a nameless "shoebox" in a police evidence locker.

Finn answered. "In warm waters, putrefaction and scavenging creatures can strip a body in as little as a couple of weeks. The sneaker, however, can survive 'til long after your future grandchildren are dead and buried. So it's possible it travelled miles: hundreds of miles even."

I felt a little queasy. In my mind I'd already conjured up an image of a sweet child, happy and smiling as she danced around in her bright pink shoes. Now I could only visualize a small, rotting corpse.

I wondered how Joshua was doing. When we were still on the boat and I had finally managed to break through the euphoria everyone else was feeling over the elephant tusks, and explain what the boy had found, his mother swept him into her arms and crooned softly to him. He had accepted her ministrations without a word, but seemed to shrink even further into his quiet shell.

Finn had immediately put a call in to Dixie and made plans for her to meet us at Marina Jack's the following morning. We could have run the boat at night and headed back to Sarasota right then, but the sun was beginning to set and Finn deemed it safer to stay at anchor overnight and make our way at first light.

Once at the marina we'd pulled into the fuel docks. There was a wait for the gas pumps, which was fine as it gave us more time with Dixie; not that there was much we could tell her about our find. Gently, Dixie asked Joshua a couple of questions then told the Bumbrys they could go. They were anxious to get their son home but promised to be in touch the next day. I gave Joshua a big hug and thanked him for educating me about fossils. His response was a tepid smile.

Dixie stayed until we'd refueled and were ready to pull away, then she grabbed the cooler that held the foot and Finn handed her off the boat.

Instead of heading back out to the Boneyard, Finn had decided to stay in Sarasota for a few days. We were able to tie up at a private slip just south of Marina Jack. The owner no longer had a boat and was happy to let us use the facilities. For us it was great because it was free. When you have to pay by the foot (no pun intended) to dock your vessel it gets expensive. *Time Voyager* is a 48-foot aluminum crew boat, retrofitted with four cabins, each with two berths, and three additional berths in the salon. She's great for salvage work, but is able to double as a cruiser – admittedly not luxury – so we could take guests out diving.

Enos and Jafet departed as soon as we'd docked. Finn had borrowed Grace Bumbry's many hours of video. He wanted to study all of the footage for evidence of slave ship wreckage, so he shut himself in his stateroom where he wouldn't be disturbed. He had dinner plans with Dixie for the evening; that left me with Shrimp, which was just fine. When we had guests onboard, I worked from sun-up to sun-down and I was looking forward to a lazy time with the TV remote and pizza delivery.

Oh, and if you haven't met Shrimp before, she's our little calico cat. We rescued her down in Key West and now, wherever *Time Voyager* goes, she goes. I used to worry that she'd get lost when we were docked at different places, but she never goes far and, somehow, always knows when we're ready to leave.

It might be a good idea as well, to explain my relationship with Finn. He's Captain Rex Finsmer, treasure hunter extraordinaire and all-around good guy. I'm

Phillida Jane Trent. Finn helped me when I was at a really low point in my life. Now he's kind of like the father figure I never had. He's one of those guys who can look a bit crusty on the outside, but he's total mush inside. Really, the most generous-hearted person I've known.

Dixie came to pick Finn up at about the same time my pizza arrived and that's when we got talking about the foot. By now I was not feeling so hungry. To change the conversation I asked Finn if he'd seen anything of interest on the videos.

"A lot of old bones; that's all. And there's still hours of footage to go."

"What are you hoping to find?" Dixie raised questioning eyebrows.

"I'll tell you over dinner," Finn said, and with that, they left.

Feeling the need for something uplifting I thumbed through our collection of movies. "Chariots of Fire." Perfect. I popped in the dvd, put the pizza in the oven to keep warm for later and opened a bottle of Dos Equis Amber. Shrimp joined me on the chair and we settled in for a feel-good evening.

Three

Three days later we headed back to the Boneyard with Enos. Jafet had a big house-painting job to finish – he and Enos are odd-jobbers in between dive gigs – and couldn't come. It would slow us down a bit but, based on the timestamp of the video, Finn had narrowed down the location of the elephant tusks. He planned to drop anchor and do a circular search. Using the anchor as a fixed reference point, he and Enos would swim around it at a set series of distances. It's tedious and time-consuming work but does ensure that the search area is completely covered.

In case you don't know, the Gulf of Mexico is like a deep bowl with a broad narrow rim. The Boneyard site is on the shallow rim, no more than 40 feet deep, so the guys were able to use the hookah – that's a surface air hose that allows diving without a tank and means the divers can stay underwater for long periods of time.

I'm a self-described weeny when it comes to being underwater. Enos kept ribbing me about it to the point where I agreed to take a turn in the search. Of course, that was when a fearsome sea monster decided to come and check out what was going on. The thing was gigantic, with an enormous mouth and beady little eyes, and it moved toward me with slow, deliberate stealth. I just knew it was thinking "lunch."

I abandoned the search and shot to the surface, but I was at least fifty feet from the boat so I started swimming and yelling for Enos who was on deck. At that moment the creature grabbed me from below. I shrieked and struggled to get away from its grasp until Finn's voice pierced my panic.

"Phill, Phill. Relax. It's OK. I've got you. It was just a jewfish." *Huh?*

Well, Finn helped me back to the boat and explained the "sea monster" was a Goliath Grouper, often called a jewfish.

"They're not usually aggressive. We might have been in his territory and he was just checking us out."

"What do you mean by 'not usually aggressive?' "

"On a rare occasion they've grabbed fish from divers who were spearfishing and the divers may have been hurt a little."

"Did you know, there's a video online of a Goliath swallowing a shark whole?" Enos was grinning. Finn gave him a "that's not very helpful" look.

"Whole?" I squeaked.

"They have a very powerful sucking system," Finn explained, "so they can swallow prey in a single gulp."

"And I was nearly prey!" This conversation wasn't reassuring me.

Finn sighed. "You just need to be alert and stay out of the way. This one was pretty small, anyway. They can get to eight feet, and this guy was half that size."

"You can bet I'm staying out of the way. That's the last time I'm going down." And I meant it.

After about a week of searching we'd found lots of fossils and a good bit of junk – chain and bits of modern-day debris, but no sign of the tusks. Finn figured at least we'd eliminated a portion of the sea bed as a wreck site, but considering the Gulf covers about 600,000 square miles I was thinking we could have a hell of a long way to go.

Anyway, Finn gave the word it was time to head in, so we set our course for Sarasota. I joined Shrimp on top of the bridge, where she liked to sun herself, and told her to hang on or she might go overboard and become jewfish fodder.

Four

Two figures were standing at our private slip as we approached. One tall and broad-shouldered; the other much shorter and slight. It was Michael Bumbry with Joshua. I looked questioningly at Finn.

"Michael called earlier and asked when we expected to get in. Other than that, I know nothing," and he shrugged his shoulders to emphasize the point.

As we drew up to the dock, Michael raised his arms. "Throw me the line."

Enos tossed him the stern line then, as Finn expertly eased *Time Voyager* into place, jumped onto the dock with the bow line and the two men quickly secured their ropes to the cleats. Finn directed Enos to shut the engines down and waved the Bumbrys aboard.

The men shook hands; I hugged Joshua. "Where's Shrimp?" he said.

As if she knew she was needed, Shrimp ambled on deck and rubbed against Joshua's legs. He picked her up and then settled himself on one of the chairs and began scratching behind her ears while he looked intently at his father. Michael gave him a slight nod.

"Finn, could we all sit down? Joshua and I have something we want to talk to you about."

This sounded serious. "Why don't I get us some iced tea, first? Joshua, I can make one of those strawberry smoothies you like."

He gave a crooked little smile that didn't reach his eyes, and nodded. "Yes, please."

When I got back with the drinks Finn was telling Michael about our search, but he stopped talking as I set the glasses down. I claimed one of the remaining chairs and we waited for Michael to begin.

"As you can imagine, we were all in a state of shock when we said our goodbyes a couple of weeks ago. Grace and I talked things through with Joshua and felt he was handling things pretty well. He's always liked to spend time on the computer, so when he shut himself in his room we figured he was researching his fossils as usual…until a few days ago." Here, Michael looked over at his son. "Why don't you explain, Joshua?"

The boy leaned forward; elbows on knees, hands clasped, his expression earnest.

"Her name's Aubrey Poulsen. There's an article that says she got lost at a festival. But she was never found and she was wearing those pink sneakers and I think she fell in the water and…"

"Hold on, son. Start at the beginning, when you decided to look for the pink shoes." Then between them, father and son explained what had brought them to us today.

Joshua had not been able to put aside the fact that there had once been a little girl who wore bright pink sneakers, and that something terrible must have happened to her. He spent hours trolling the internet until he finally found a reference to a child who had gone missing while vacationing with her parents in Belize. According to the brief police report the family had been at the San Pedro festival, with thousands of other people, when Aubrey went missing. She was described as a brown-haired, brown-eyed ten-year-old, wearing a flower patterned T-shirt, yellow shorts and bright pink air sneakers.

"Although I write fiction novels now," Michael stated, "I used to be an investigative reporter. I managed to track down Aubrey's mother and spoke with her on the phone. She lives now in Austin, Texas. She was very willing to talk and sent me information from a private investigator she and her husband hired in Belize.

"Hand it to Finn, son," he said to Joshua, who held out a slightly battered blue folder.

Peering over Finn's shoulder, in large letters on the cover I read, *Aubrey Poulsen*. Beneath, in smaller letters, was *daughter of Pipaluk (Luki) and Lenard*.

"Luki?" I queried.

"It's pronounced 'Lucky.' She's part Native American."

Finn opened the file and an eight by ten picture filled the page. The face that gazed out at us was the color of warm golden sand. Dark hair had been pulled into a single braid and lay across one shoulder. The lips were closed in a shy smile that emphasized high cheek bones and lit up her dark eyes. She looked so alive. She looked like a child who should have a happy and bright future ahead of her.

With a sigh, Finn gently closed the cover and I knew he was thinking as I was. "Keep talking," he said to Michael.

"There's not a lot. The police pretty much dismissed it as a child wandering off. They had bigger things on their hands at the time. A rare Maya artifact had been stolen from the museum and, for them, that took precedence over parents who couldn't keep track of their daughter.

"The investigator, a local named Doren Gillett, appears to have made an honest effort to locate Aubrey. You'll see from the notes in the file he questioned a lot of people, flyers were posted, ads put in the newspaper, a reward was offered, but not a single lead came of it all.

"Here's what makes the story even sadder. The father blamed himself for Aubrey's disappearance, started drinking heavily and a few months ago stepped off the sidewalk in front of a truck and was killed."

"Suicide?" Finn asked.

"There's really no way to know. He was drunk at the time and could have just slipped. Or maybe he couldn't take the guilt any more. Meanwhile, Luki told me she is broke because they spent all their money looking for Aubrey."

For a few moments there was silence, then Finn spoke. "It's a terrible story, but what do you want of me?"

"To find out what happened."

It was Joshua who had chimed in. We all looked at him. "You're good at finding things; everyone says so."

"It's not that simple." Finn for once looked a little helpless.

"Look," Michael got to his feet and began pacing, "when Joshua first brought this up I figured he'd forget about it after a while, but he hasn't. In fact, he's been having nightmares lately. So Grace and I have talked things over and we feel we can't just let this go. We don't have a lot saved up, but my books are starting to do well and we have enough to get you to Belize with a little payment for your services."

Astonished, Finn shook his head. "Michael, any evidence is ice cold by now. And why would you think I can do more than the local police and investigator? I've never even been to Belize. You'd be wasting your money, I'm afraid."

"You've worked miracles before, when cases are cold." *He had a point there.*

"Please, Finn," Michael's small voice broke in.

"Here's what I'll do," Finn said. "We'll be taking *Time Voyager* back to Mud Bug Island in the next couple of days. Once we get there I'll go over everything in the file and let you know what I think."

A smile creased Joshua's face. Finn turned to him. "I'm not promising anything, young man."

"OK, Finn," the boy said, still smiling.

Five

"And that's everything we know." I looked at Bert as I set my beer down and leaned back in the chair. Bert is Elbert Lex Van Nifterik, the young multi-millionaire entrepreneur who owns Mud Bug Island off the west Florida coast. Owing to Bert's generosity, Mud Bug is now *Time Voyager's* home base. In return for free dockage, Bert likes to involve himself in our adventures, which is an even better deal for me and Finn as Bert is a genius on the computer.

So, here we were, on the patio of Bert's home, talking about a dead body. There was a surreal quality to the conversation because, not so long before, a body had been found on that very same patio. In fact, it was after Finn solved the crime that Bert had offered us a mooring.

"I think you should go." Bert emphasized his words with a brief nod of the head.

Finn sighed. "It doesn't appear as if a crime was committed and, a year later, I don't see how I can find out more about a missing child than the local authorities did at the time."

"But that's the point," I said, "the police really didn't look."

"Phill, I know you want to help Joshua; so do I. You have to keep in mind, though, it may be a dead end and then the boy will be even more disappointed and we'll have wasted the Bumbry's money for nothing."

"Isn't that for Michael and Grace to decide?" I was beginning to sulk.

"Not if you don't use their money," Bert said. We both turned to him.

"I want in on this search. Unfortunately, I can't actually go myself; I have to be in California this coming week for the unveiling of my latest game." Amongst other things, Bert created pirate-themed video games. "However, I can certainly afford to pay for both of you, and Michael, to go to Belize. You'll have to fly commercial, though. I'll be using the jet myself."

"Jet? What jet?" This was the first I'd heard of Bert owning a jet.

"It's just a Learjet 60. I'm thinking of trading it for something a little bigger. This doesn't have quite enough range to get to San Francisco without stopping to refuel."

Wow. I should consider trading treasure hunting for the video gaming business.

With Bert's urging, it didn't take long for Finn to agree to the trip. We looked up flights from Miami to Belize City and found several options, so called Michael to discuss times.

"The sooner the better," he said and we booked ourselves on a nonstop flight with American Airlines for the day after tomorrow. Business class, I might add, at Bert's insistence.

"Now that's taken care of," Finn said, "just for the heck of it I'd like to get as much information as possible about the theft that was keeping the Belizean police so busy."

"You think there's a connection?"

"Unlikely, but let's be sure."

Bert stood. "I can take care of that. You and Phill need time to get yourselves organized."

"There's not much…" I began, then was struck with a thought. "Who will take care of Shrimp?"

"That would be me," a very British voice said.

Monks, who is Bert's butler and bodyguard, stepped onto the patio to collect our empty glasses.

"You're not going with Bert?"

"Apparently, arrangements have been made by the video company for Bert's protection, and I am to stay here and oversee installation of an upgraded security system."

"You're the only one I can trust," Bert shrugged.

Actually, there was more truth to that than you might know. Monks was the only full-time staff living on the island. Twice a week a cleaning service came over, and other help was brought in as needed. A gourmet meal service shipped to the island monthly and the food was stored in a large walk-in freezer. Everything was designed to maintain the privacy Bert embraced. Finn and I were pretty privileged to be a part of the young man's "family."

"Monks, you're a prince," I said. "Don't overdo the treats, though. I don't want her getting chunky."

"That won't be a problem with Bert away." Monks sent a knowing look in his employer's direction. Bert stuffed his hands in his pockets, "Uh, I'll go search for that information," and headed indoors.

I directed my attention to Monks. "I didn't think Bert was much of a cat fan."

"Huh. We now have a standing order for 20 pounds of shrimp a month to ensure your cat will never be deprived of her favorite crustacean."

Good grief.

"Alright." Finn directed his words to me. "Let's go figure out what we need to take with us. I hope your passport's in order."

"Absolutely!" *But where had I put it?*

Six

We were staying at the Radisson Fort George Hotel on Belize City's Caribbean coast. Bert had done us proud. The hotel was definitely deluxe, with its own marina and dive facilities and a really well-stocked bar. We were just half a mile from downtown, and only an hour by fast boat to Ambergris Caye.

I wondered if we'd have any chance to explore the area. The Maya first settled in Belize around 1500 BC. Europeans didn't make their homes here until the 1600s when the English arrived. As you can imagine, there's an amazing blend of cultures and lots to see and do. *I could also enjoy zip lining through the tropical forest or river tubing through Maya caves.*

It was late afternoon when we reached the hotel. Belize City is an hour behind Florida time during the winter months so, for us, it was cocktail hour. However, anxious to make a start, Finn had called the PI, Doren Gillett, the moment he hit his room and had arranged for us to meet at some place called Nerie's Restaurant, where we could talk over dinner.

Michael joined us in the hotel lobby. It was less than a ten minute walk to the restaurant, and after hours of traveling we were glad to stretch our legs a little. Nerie's was in a dumpy neighborhood in a very unpretentious corner building with one of those old-fashioned, red Coca

Cola signs hanging from the side. It looked as if we were about to get a taste of local experience.

We were greeted warmly, but when Finn announced we were to meet Doren Gillett the friendliness quotient went even higher. Apparently any friend of Gillett's was a friend at Nerie's. Ushered to a discreetly located table our host stated that Gillett had not yet arrived and suggested we enjoy a bottle of the local Belikin beer while we waited.

"Sounds good to me," Finn said.

Before the brews arrived a dark-skinned man entered. He had close-cropped hair and van dyke beard. He hesitated and looked around. As soon as he noticed us he moved in our direction. I nudged Finn. "Looks like our guy."

We all rose and exchanged handshakes and polite greetings. Gillett spoke with a very proper English accent and was much younger than I'd expected. I'd automatically envisioned the kind of hard-boiled, older guy you get in a lot of detective stories, but Gillett was no more than early thirties.

"You don't sound Belizean," I said.

His mouth formed a lop-sided grin. *Sexy.* "That's because I'm British by birth, though my heritage is African-Caribbean. Any ethnic accent I might have had was long gone after years of private schooling and then three years at Oxford."

Michael propped his elbows on the table. "Oxford University? I'm impressed. What did you study?"

"Mathematics."

"But here you are as a private eye in Belize."

Doren smiled again. It was very infectious; he was definitely easy on the eyes. "After Oxford I wanted to travel. I went through Europe, South America, even Nepal. When I came here I fell in love with the country. That was three years ago. Currently I have permanent residency status; in a couple more years I will be able to apply for citizenship."

"But why detective work?"

"I'm a mathematician; I like detail. And it beats the hell out of bussing tables."

"Tell us how you came to work for the Poulsens."

Finn coughed and cast an apologetic look toward Michael. "Can I make a suggestion? How about we eat and then get down to serious business?"

That certainly suited me. I'm always ready to eat.

We chowed on conch soup with sides of coconut rice and beans, washed down with more Belikin. Conversation remained light, Doren entertaining us with stories of his adopted country. When we were all sated and the dishes had been cleared we automatically looked to Finn to take charge.

"Alrighty, then. Doren, we've all read the summation of your investigation that you sent to Mrs. Poulsen, but I'd like to hear it in your own words. Especially anything that wasn't in the report."

"There's really nothing much I can add. I'd only been in business a few weeks, hadn't had anything more exciting than looking for a lost cat or two. When the

Poulsens came along I was thrilled. Don't misunderstand, the circumstances were tragic but I was thankful to be looking for a real person instead of a wandering pet.

"At first I was convinced the child had simply got lost at the San Pedro festival. Thousands of people attend and someone must have seen her. The parents gave a description of her wearing sunflower yellow shorts and neon pink sneakers. She was hardly inconspicuous.

"I posted dozens of flyers all over the island, distributed hundreds more and talked to more people than I could say but not one person came forward with information. I ran ads in local publications, persuaded them to feature articles about Aubrey and still there was nothing."

"Do you think the theft of Maya jade from the Belize Museum hampered your search?" Michael asked.

"You're suggesting the publicity about the theft detracted from interest in a child's disappearance?"

Michael nodded.

"There's no doubt it made a difference in the police investigation, but I can't say it impacted mine. In fact, it became very personal for me. I would look at Aubrey's picture and imagine this sweet little girl afraid and lost and I'd redouble my efforts. Long after the Poulsens left here I kept looking. I extended my search far beyond Ambergris Caye, hoping all the time that I might one day pick up the phone and say, 'I've found her.' "

"And there was nothing at all that struck you as odd?"

Doren ran his hand through his short hair and leaned back, closing his eyes for a moment. "Well, yes there was. The Poulsens took the water taxi from the city Marine Terminal to San Pedro. I interviewed everyone I could find at the San Pedro docks and there was one old Kriol, a local chap, who spends his days hanging around fishing and people watching and he absolutely swore the girl had not got off any of the water taxis."

"That's hardly surprising," I said. "An old man, thousands of tourists…"

"I know. But several people told me he was the guy to talk to, and he was so emphatic it really struck me. That's not all, though. When I widened my search to Belize City - even got a couple of minutes to make an appeal on a local TV news show - suddenly, several people contacted me saying they recalled seeing Aubrey around the Terminal. Now *that* seemed strange."

Finn chewed his bottom lip and nodded thoughtfully. "I agree. She was memorable in Belize City but not San Pedro. Makes a person wonder if she ever got to the island. Did anybody recall who Aubrey was with when they saw her?"

"Just vague references to a women who it was assumed was her mother. One person thought she was with both parents."

"What are you thinking, Finn?" Michael asked.

"I'm thinking we need a good night's sleep so we can be ready to fight another day."

"No, I mean about…" Michael began when I interrupted him.

"Don't waste your breath. He's got an idea about something but you won't get anything out of him 'til he's ready." *I'd had plenty of experience.*

That said, we let Finn take charge of the check, said all the usual stuff to Doren about staying in touch and letting us know if he thought of anything else, and departed for our hotel.

Seven

Ambergris Caye is the largest of the Belizean islands and San Pedro is the only town. Fishing and coconuts are traditional ways of earning a living but now take a back seat to diving and tourism.

Finn, Michael and I had cast off from the Radisson marina at about nine in the morning. The hotel had arranged rental of a 25-foot Aquasport Osprey for the day and we'd set out to follow the course the Poulsens must have taken.

We'd taken our time on the outward journey. Finn wanted to check the other Cayes as we passed. When I asked him what he was looking for, he just said, "I'll know it if I see it." *Typical*.

Hicks Caye appeared to have only private residential properties. Finn drove slowly by without stopping. We detoured slightly to Long Caye but that, too, was fairly barren of property and activity.

Next was Caye Chapel to the east.

"This is privately owned," Michael said, then noticed my questioning look. "I checked a few things out on the internet last night. There's a resort on the island with a golf course and an airstrip for small planes. It was bank owned and had been on the selling block for a long time, but looks to have just sold to a Mexican hotel development group."

Finn looked interested. "Does that mean the property was abandoned?"

"From what I could tell the golf course was open but not the resort. So I would imagine there were a few staff living there."

"Was the bank in possession when Aubrey went missing?"

"I believe they were."

I turned to Finn and gave him my "What?" look, but as usual he ignored me.

On we went to Caye Caulker, dropping in behind one of the sleek water taxis that runs between Belize City, Caye Caulker and San Pedro, and dogging it to its terminal. Instead of pulling in there, Finn continued slowly north along the shoreline. "We're looking for the Rainbow Grill," he told us.

"I don't know about you," I glanced at Michael, "but I could go for a snack."

"We're not here to eat, but the restaurant is central to the main street and we can dock at their jetty and take a quick look around the town. Ah, here it is."

Finn turned toward the beach and in a few minutes we were tied up and walking along the jetty to the restaurant, a bright blue clapboard affair on stilts. They were obviously not yet open but there was a man on the deck wiping down tables. As we approached he gave a cheery wave, "Gud mawnin," and told us they wouldn't be open for another hour. Finn asked if it was OK to dock there for a while.

"Aarite," our pal nodded enthusiastically, "evryting gud."

We took that for a "yes" and strolled onto the sand road.

The town pretty much consisted of Front Street, Middle Street and Back Street. Buildings were a kaleidoscopic blend of pink, turquoise, sunny yellow and sea foam green with white-fenced porches and rooftop gardens. There were plenty of quaint, if touristy, shops and restaurants.

Michael was business-like. "Do you mind explaining what we're doing here, Finn?"

"Let's just take a little time to talk to some of the locals and see if anyone here saw the Poulsens."

"Why?" I asked.

"Just trying to get as much information as possible. The water taxi stops here on its way to San Pedro. Just maybe the Poulsens got off for a while. We've got damn little to go on, so even if we eliminate possibilities it will help. I brought some of Doren's flyers," he pulled out a wad of folded papers from a pocket, "to show around."

"Well, I guess it won't hurt." Michael held out his hand for a copy. Resignedly, I did the same and we split up.

An hour later we were back together, all with the same story. No luck.

"Alrighty, then," Finn said, "time to move on to San Pedro."

The Rainbow Grill had still not opened, though there was more activity as staff prepped for the lunch crowd. We merely walked on by to board our rental when it occurred to me we hadn't shown Aubrey's picture to anyone at the Grill.

"Hold on!" I yelled, and dashed back waving my flyer in the air.

"Do any of you remember seeing this girl last year during the San Pedro festival?"

"I might have," a voice said and I turned in surprise to a serious-faced woman.

"Here? On Caye Caulker?"

She ducked her chin. "A group of us were going to the festival. We were in a friend's boat, but I remember because I have a daughter about that age. She was the one who saw her and she liked the girl's outfit. She went on and on at me to get her something like it."

"Where did you see her?"

"We were just getting on the boat – a bit south of here, as a matter of fact, by the water taxi, and that's where we saw her."

"On the taxi?"

"Getting off. It was a bit odd, now I think about it. They got off the taxi and then straight on another boat."

"Who's they?"

"A woman. She was holding her hand."

"Did you see anyone else with her? Anyone in the boat?"

"No, I'm sorry. I didn't pay attention."

Though I tried to wring more information from her that was all the woman had. Still, I strode back to the others feeling pretty pleased with myself.

San Pedro was a larger version of Caye Caulker. With more of a bustling atmosphere it was still very much a shorts and sandals place. Eateries and beach bars ribboned the Caribbean waters while tourists and locals alike ambled along the streets or cruised by on bikes and in golf carts.

"I take it we'll be showing Aubrey's picture around again," I said to Finn.

"Right. You and Michael make a start in the shops. I'm going to see if I can find the old guy that the private eye mentioned, so I'll hang around the docks for now." He looked up and down the sand road. "Then let's meet there for lunch."

He gestured toward a red-trimmed, yellow building with an invitingly shady porch, above which hung a sign, Licks Beachside Café.

"Works for me," I said as Michael gave his assent.

Finn wandered away and Michael and I decided our best course of action was to each take one side of the street. Michael opted for the beach side, which was mostly restaurants, while I popped in and out of small stores selling everything from local artwork, jewelry, souvenirs, edibles and colorful clothing.

Fortunately, I'm not into clothes or jewelry, otherwise it could have been very distracting. Everyone I talked with was friendly. A number of people remembered Doren asking about Aubrey a year ago, and all of them had the same answer: they had no recollection of the little girl with pink sneakers.

By the time we met at Licks I was ready for a break – and hungry. The place was packed but Mario, the owner, set up a table on the beach for us. Three bottles of Belikin were soon in hand – I was really beginning to like this beer – and though I was tempted by the curry coconut conch, once again we all ordered the same thing, bacon cheese hamburger. *Delicious.*

As we ate we discussed what we knew so far. It wasn't much. Finn had found the old fisherman exactly where Doren had told him to look, and the man was more than willing to talk.

"Willing didn't make it easy though. Jack's a character and speaks in a mix of his native Kriol and heavily accented English. If circumstances were different ah mi gat wahn gud taim wid heem."

What?

Seeing our puzzled expressions, Finn explained. "I'd have a good time with him. At least, I think that's what I said."

Michael rolled his eyes and Finn got serious again.

"No matter how I asked the questions, Jack didn't waver from his assertion that Aubrey never arrived here. And I have to tell you, he's sharp as they come with a

42

memory like a steel trap. He claims to recall seeing Lenard and Pipaluk Poulsen, not just from the description Doren gave him, but says he noticed them because Lenard had a bloody lip and was acting strangely."

Michael frowned. "Our PI friend didn't mention that."

At the same time I said, "Strangely, how so?"

Finn looked from one to the other of us. "Jack said Lenard seemed like a man going to a funeral rather than someone looking forward to a fun vacation day. He also is quite sure they did not get off the water taxi."

"What does that mean?"

"If it's true, it means they must have arrived on a private boat."

I sighed. "We don't seem to be getting anywhere fast."

"Maybe we'll learn something more in a while," Finn said. "After I finished with my new friend I put a call in to the San Pedro Police substation. We're meeting Chief Benjamin Flowers in about an hour."

"How did you manage that?" Michael asked.

"Dixie called and asked for his cooperation."

"You mean Detective Tanner in Sarasota?"

Finn nodded as he took a long pull at his beer. "The same. So let's finish our meal and find our way to the police station."

Eight

There was no fear of missing the police station. The two-story building was canary yellow with green trim. From a balcony above the main entrance hung a sign that read "SAN PEDRO POLICE STATION." A bright red police pick-up was parked in front.

Inside, it was certainly no bastion of modernity or technology. The officers were all smart enough in their tan shirts and navy pants but the word that came to mind as I looked around was "basic." I'd say there was a serious lack of funding for the local constabulary.

Anyway, the desk was being managed by Sergeant Garbutt, who requested to know our business politely enough. We asked for and were promptly taken to Chief Flowers. He was an overly avuncular man, all hearty and jolly, which seemed out of place. I wondered if that was indicative of the way he handled police work. He offered refreshments, which we declined and Finn got right to business, explaining our purpose and asking if there was anything the Chief could add to the original investigation. Immediately, Flower's expression morphed into one of melancholy and he steepled his fingers together beneath his chin. Again, his attitude struck me as somewhat fake.

"Captain, I am very much saddened at this disappearance of a little girl. I must tell you, I was not in

San Pedro at the time. I have been chief here for only six months."

"I'm aware it was Chief Moody who was in charge then and I hope to be able to talk with him at some time. Meanwhile, you're the man I hope will have some insight."

"Ah, your wish to speak with Chief Colin Moody will not, I fear, be possible. He retired and moved to the mountains but a slip on a mountain path, a broken neck…" Here he gave a thumbs-down. "When the lady detective called from America, I myself looked into the files and I assure you, a thorough investigation was made."

"But the child still wasn't found."

Flowers dismissively waved a hand. "There was no verification that she ever arrived on the island, and the police cannot be responsible for all the parents who do not have proper control over their children."

"What the hell." Michael sat up straight. "First you say there was an investigation, then you blame the parents. What is it?"

Flowers' lips drew into a thin line and Finn jumped in to smooth the waters. "I'm sure everything possible was done. It must have been difficult with so many tourists on the island, and I imagine you were also participating in the search for the men who robbed the museum."

"That is so. They took a priceless piece of Belizean history. We were alerted to watch for unusual boat traffic or suspicious persons arriving. It was speculated the thieves might try and hand off the relic under cover of the festivities. So you see," he threw a stern look in Michael's direction, "it was even more likely the girl would have been spotted if she was here."

After that, Flowers became generally uncooperative. He refused Finn's request to look through the files and very soon dismissed us, saying he had another, important, appointment.

"Could a day be more unproductive?" Michael was glum.

"I wouldn't say that." Finn started walking back to the boat dock and Michael and I stepped in beside him.

"It almost seemed like Flowers was being deliberately obstructive." I wasn't feeling too positive myself.

"I wouldn't disagree, though he's right they would have been on high alert and perhaps more likely to notice the child."

"Then what's our next move?"

"We'll work on that when we get back to the hotel."

We made it back to the Radisson in barely an hour. We were all pretty weary so decided to clean up and then mosey over to Nerie's and talk over dinner and a few brews. Michael wanted to call his family and said he'd catch up in a while. So Finn and I strolled off.

The streets were pretty quiet. As we approached the restaurant we noticed a couple of guys hanging about the sidewalk. They were both wearing caps pulled low and smoking. I didn't think anything of it but Finn said "Let's cross to the other side." Dutifully I followed as he stepped into the street. Both of us looked back for any traffic. As we did, two other guys rushed us from behind. At the same time the first two tossed aside their cigarettes and ran towards us. They didn't look like a rescue party.

Trapped in the middle I was looking for anything I could use as a weapon when I realized Finn had charged the first two men. Shoulder down he barreled into them, knocking one guy flying.

"Run," he yelled as he managed to land a blow on the other ruffian before the first jumped back up and got him in a choke hold. Instead, I dashed to him and kicked the guy viciously behind the knee. He sank down but managed to keep his hold on Finn. The other two were almost on us.

"Get help." Finn's eyes sought mine and pleaded. "Go!"

The third thug stretched forward and grabbed my upper arm and I was galvanized into action. I swung inward to face him, bringing my free arm up to grab his dreadlocks. Yanking his head down hard I simultaneously brought my knee up and smashed his nose. He screamed and released me and I dodged away.

At that moment an old van pulled into the street. With a screech it braked beside us. The side door opened and another guy jumped out. Between them they hauled Finn and the injured man inside while one of them held a knife at me. I backed away. Heroics would likely get me dead, and that wouldn't help anyone. Instead, I did my best to memorize faces and the van before it tore off. Then I rushed to Nerie's screaming blue murder and demanding the police.

Nine

"Phill. Wake up!"

I jerked upright and pain spasmed down my neck. My head ached and my mouth felt dry and tacky. "Coffee. I need coffee," I mumbled. Then I remembered where I was and why.

Finn lay in a hospital bed; I'd been slumped over in one of those ridiculously uncomfortable chairs they insist on furnishing for visitors. Michael was gently shaking my shoulder. "It's more like tea time," he said. "Four in the afternoon."

I glanced at Finn. He was so still but I could see a slight rise and fall of the bedsheet in rhythm with his breathing. "Any improvement?"

"The doctor says he'll have a hell of a headache but there should be no lasting effects. They're expecting him to come out of it soon, and Inspector Usher is on his way. Why don't you go and freshen up a bit and grab something to eat. I'll stay here and keep an eye on him."

"OK, but I'll just run to the restroom. I want to be here when he wakes."

I dragged myself to the ladies' bathroom and splashed cold water over my face. My mouth tasted as if something had decayed in it. So I rubbed a little of the floral antiseptic soap from the wall dispenser across my teeth with my finger. It was almost worse than before. I swished it out as best I could but the taste remained. Oh, well. At least my breath would be attractive, which was more than could be said for the bloodshot eyes staring back at me in the mirror as I recalled events of the previous evening.

The Belize City police had arrived at Nerie's with surprising speed. I'd grabbed a note pad from a server and already written down everything I could remember about the kidnappers, which wasn't much. Michael had arrived just after the police. Together we waited at the local police station, alternately pacing around the reception area.

It was suggested that Finn might have been targeted for a ransom. I clung to that hope because all the other alternatives that sprang to mind were much worse. In case money was needed, I called Bert in California. He was on it immediately, and promised he'd be ready to send funds any time.

"Look, I can scratch this conference and come down there right now," he'd said.

I blinked back tears – you know how it is when times are tough and people are really nice. "You're a prince, Bert. Let's see how this plays out tonight first, but can I take a raincheck on that?"

"You bet, Phill. I'm here for you guys."

I'd had the speakerphone on so that Michael could listen in. As I ended the call he stuffed his hands in his jeans pockets and faced me. "Let's call the PI, Doren Gillett, in on this. There may be people who will talk to him before the police."

By then it was about eleven in the evening but Gillett answered immediately. Together, Michael and I gave him all the details. We agreed, no matter what, we'd check in with each other in a couple of hours.

The waiting was killer; I felt so helpless. For the heck of it I called Detective Dixie back in Sarasota. I had no idea what she might possibly do to help but at least I was calling in every hand I could. Dixie didn't answer so I left a message. A few minutes later she called back.

"Phill, I'm almost afraid to know why you called because it can't be good."

I gave her the rundown. "I know there's really nothing you can do, but I figured you'd want to be kept up-to-date on what's happening."

Dixie had been concerned and sympathetic, and asked a lot of questions as any good cop should. "I was getting ready for an early night with a good book when you called. What I'm going to do instead is head to the station and make another official call to police in Belize. Likely, it won't do much. But it won't hurt to elevate Finn's importance and let them know we have an interest."

"You're the best, Dixie."

When Gillett called at the appointed hour there was still no news. A couple of people had admitted seeing the van race off but if they had any idea who was in it they weren't saying. The PI told us he would continue canvassing the area. For our part, Michael and I had continually bugged the lone duty officer for updates, but none were forthcoming.

At precisely two twelve in the morning the station phone rang. The desk officer lifted it from its cradle and spoke indifferently into the mouthpiece. Michael and I both tensed and strained to listen. Suddenly the officer became animated. He punched buttons and spoke rapidly to some unseen person. My cell buzzed. I looked at the display and mouthed "Gillett" to Michael as I hit answer.

"There's something going on here." As I said it a black Ford police truck screamed from behind the building, lights flashing. I heard Michael yell, "Where are they going?"

"Doren, I have to call you back."

"No, wait. Wait. It's me."

"What?" I had no idea what he meant but he certainly was excited about something.

"It's me on the other line with the police department. He's here. Finn is here. They dumped him back near the restaurant."

I was shocked into momentary silence. When I found my voice it came out in a shriek. "Is he OK?"

"He's unconscious," *Oh, God,* "but he's alive."

So here I was hanging over the bathroom sink when there was knock on the door.

"Phill."

I yanked the door open. "What's happened, Michael?"

"The doctor's going to wake him so he'll be able to talk to the inspector."

We hurried back to the room. This was a different doctor than the one who'd examined him on arrival and he introduced himself as Doctor Cawich. "I've just given him a mild stimulative. He'll come around slowly but may be a bit confused, so it would be a good idea if yours is the first face he sees." *Good, 'cause that's what I intended anyway.*

When Finn's eyes blinked open they looked straight into mine. "Hi, honey," he said and I wanted to weep with relief. Instead, I kept my big girl pants on and feigned annoyance. "Holy shit, you'll do almost anything for attention." Then I explained to him he was at a private clinic.

"That sounds expensive."

"Bert's taking care of everything. We didn't want you in a government-run hospital." They're decidedly less than state of the art. "Here you have a private room and a nurse dedicated to your care."

Finn's eyebrows lifted. "Is she pretty?"

"Well, she's a he, sooo…"

His face fell and I took pity on him. "If it makes you feel better, Dixie sends her love."

A slight smile brightened his features.

I turned to Michael and the doctor. "He's just fine."

Ten

Inspector Antoine Usher was pencil thin with a pencil thin mustache, and he seriously reminded me of an older Little Richard without all the hair. His manner was far removed from a flamboyant rock star, however, as he held out an arm in greeting to Finn.

"I hope you're feeling better," he said.

"Thanks. I'm ready to leave but the doctor – and some other people," he glared at me, "are insisting I stay tonight."

"You got a nasty crack on the head," I narrowed my eyes back at him. "It's for your own good."

"You were beaten?" Little Richard…I mean Usher, gave a questioning look.

"I smacked my head when they pushed me out of the van. Gave myself a bit of a concussion, that's all." Finn dismissed his injury.

"Start from the time you were snatched, Captain." Usher grabbed the single chair and seated himself next to the bed. "Constable Mejia will take notes." He cocked his head to the young policewoman who accompanied him, then looked expectantly at Finn.

"They stuck a rag over my face that was damped with starter fluid."

"Starter fluid?" Michael frowned and Usher responded in the sort of voice a teacher might use to a particularly dense student.

"It's readily available for automotive use and it's also used to get high. It contains diethyl ether and some other very nasty chemicals. Dealers sell a distilled version on the streets they claim is safe but there's no such thing. It can cause permanent brain damage."

"It's definitely an experience I never want to repeat, though they only used enough to disorient me. And it worked. I have no idea where I was taken. My first clear memory is being strapped to a chair with a hood over my head. I never saw any faces; I never saw anything. Only one man spoke. He had a heavy accent that was hard to understand."

"What sort of accent?" The inspector interrupted.

"Uuuh, Kriol but with a good dose of, um, what do you call it? African-based."

"Garifuna?"

"Yeah, I think that's it."

"And what did this man say?" Usher asked.

"He was asking me questions about the jade that was stolen from the museum."

Usher's brow furrowed and his tone became hard. "Why would he think you'd know anything about that?"

"I couldn't tell you! We came down here to find out what happened to a lost little girl. The only thing the two incidents have in common as far as I can see is that they happened about the same time. For some reason, the guy seemed to think we were here to look for the jade."

Usher's questions continued until the doctor announced it was enough, and Finn needed to rest.

"We'll be talking again," the inspector said before he exited.

I watched the inspector disappear then turned to Finn and stood with hands on hips. "Come on. Out with it."

"There's nothing to come out with."

Michael and I looked at each other in disbelief, then back at Finn.

"Seriously," he went on, "the guy struck me as being genuinely surprised I wasn't interested in the jade. If he hadn't believed me, I'm not so sure I'd be talking to you right now."

"Let me get this straight," Michael said. "You got kidnapped because the hoodlums thought we were after the Maya jade that was stolen from the museum. What have we done that could possibly make them think that?"

Before there was time to respond a young woman came in, pushing a cart ahead of her. Her skin was on the dark side of copper. The smile she gave Finn was reflected in obsidian eyes as she greeted him. "Hi. It's dinner time, Mr. Finsmer."

"Who are you?"

"I'm your nurse, Kellee."

"I thought I had a male nurse."

"That was Jamaal. He was your day nurse. I'll be with you all night. Here, let me help you sit up so you can eat."

She leaned over Finn, putting her arms around his waist to help him into a sitting position. Over her shoulder he looked at me with a triumphant grin.

"You're obviously in good hands," I said in a sarcastic tone. "I'm going back to the hotel. A hot shower and a good night's sleep sound really good right now."

"Agreed," said Michael, and together we left.

Eleven

Walking through the Radisson lobby we heard a sudden shout. "Phill. Michael."

Doren Gillett stepped from the bar. "I've been watching for you. How's Finn?"

"He's fine, all things considered. Why didn't you just come to the clinic?"

"I did. They wouldn't let me in to see him and I didn't want to bother you guys; you had enough on your minds. I've been calling the hotel to see if you were back, then decided I'd come and hang out for a while and hope I got lucky. And I did, because here you are."

We exchanged a few words then Doren asked, "Have you guys eaten? Can I buy you dinner and we can talk more?"

Michael excused himself. "I think I'm going to order in-room and have a long video-chat with my wife and son."

As tired as I was, it occurred to me I was really hungry. And there were much worse things than having dinner with an attractive man.

"If you don't mind waiting another twenty minutes so I can clean up, I'll be glad to join you."

So that's how it went. Doren and I sat together at a window table in the hotel dining room.

"We could have just stayed in the bar," I said.

"This is much nicer," he smiled at me, "and more private."

After a couple of cold Belikins and the seafood combo I was feeling much better and conversation turned to recent events.

"Do you have any idea why Finn was targeted?" I asked Doren.

"Most foreigners think of Belize and think sun-drenched beaches and clear blue waters, but the country is ranked among the top ten in the world for homicides. Drugs, money laundering, human trafficking, organized crime, corruption – they're all significant problems."

"So you're saying there could be a million reasons why this happened?"

"Pretty much."

"Then why did the gangsters keep asking about the jade?"

"You've got me there. Nothing in my investigation led me to suspect any link between Aubrey's disappearance and the theft."

I yawned. "Sorry, Doren. This has been a long couple of days. I'm gonna have to say good-night."

He jumped up to help me out of my chair, which was a good thing as I slipped right into his arms. My heart-rate immediately sped up and I knew my face must be red. I hoped to God he didn't notice.

"Perhaps I'd better see you to your room," he said.

Arm in arm we made our way to my door. I was hotly aware of his body as we walked. Was he going to make a pass at me? I tried to act nonchalant as he took my room key and unlocked the door. He leaned towards me – *this is it, he's going to kiss me* – and pushed open the door behind me. Then he held out the key saying, "Goodnight," and walked away.

Well, shit.

Twelve

At nine in the morning Michael and I were at the clinic to collect Finn. He had been all for walking to the Radisson but, though he looked good and insisted he felt great, I was like an over-protective parent and insisted we ride the short distance. Michael paid off the taxi and we entered the hotel. The desk clerk hailed us as we walked by and the manager came out from his office.

"Welcome back, Captain. We're all very thankful you're OK."

Finn accepted the good wishes with a smile.

"There is an important message here for you." The manager snapped his fingers at the clerk who promptly handed over an envelope. "Russell Longsworth, who is the Director of the Museum of Belize, has requested that you meet as soon as possible."

Finn ripped open the envelope and pulled out a single sheet of paper. "It doesn't say anything more here except it's urgent, and he gives his private number."

"I wonder what it's about," I said.

"We'll find out soon," Finn replied. "I'll call when we get to the room."

The Museum of Belize was a former prison. Entry to the two story building was through the original archway, barred by iron gates that were now open to allow the paying public to pass through. At the ticket office we announced ourselves and were directed to a door marked "Private." As we closed it behind us another door opened and Russell Longsworth appeared. I'd looked him up online and easily recognized the thin face and thick-lensed glasses. He shook Finn's hand, then clasped mine and I was struck by how soft and smooth his own hands were.

At Finn's request Michael had stayed behind to coordinate some online research with Bert and Dixie. Of course, when we asked Finn why he wanted the information he was his usual vague self.

Anyway, Longsworth led us to a brick-walled office furnished in utilitarian style and we settled into straight-back chairs and waited for him to enlighten us.

"I've heard about your mishap, Captain. Are you well now?" *Mishap? That's an understatement.* Without waiting for Finn's reply he continued, "Would you like some coffee, or an aperitif? I have some local soursop wine?"

We both hurriedly declined. I had no idea what soursop wine was but it didn't sound too tasty. I later found out soursop is a fruit and the wine has flavors of pineapple and citrus. Then I wished I'd tried it.

"You're probably wondering why I asked you to meet." The Director shuffled papers on his desk then cleared his throat and took a deep breath. "I have a proposition for you."

I was startled but did my best to follow Finn's lead and remain impassive.

"Go on," Finn said.

"Perhaps it would be better if I show you something first." Longsworth practically leapt from his chair and strode to the door. "Follow me, please."

It was more command than request, and Finn and I hurried to keep pace as we were led into the heart of the museum.

Longsworth stopped at a reinforced glass case in which a carved jade head was displayed. We waited while a small group of school girls in white uniforms passed by. The Director patted the top of the case. "This is a replica, of course."

Puzzled, Finn and I just looked at him.

"…Of the Maya jade head that was stolen last year. The carving is the most important artifact the people of Belize have ever owned. Its value is priceless."

Finn and I peered through the glass as the Director gushed on. "It dates back to at least 600 B.C. See the crossed eyes and fang-like elements, these represent Kinich Ahau, the Maya sun god. The true artifact would have been carved using stones and taken years to create. The work is exquisite."

"I get that," Finn said, "but just why are we here?"

"Because we want you to find it, of course." Longsworth's brow furrowed as if he couldn't believe we were so dense that we had to ask. "You're already looking for it, and the Museum has authorized me to offer a very generous sum for its recovery."

Finn threw his hands up in the air. "For the last time, I am not searching for the jade. I'm only interested in finding out what happened to a little girl."

Longsworth's jaw dropped. "Oh… I understood…um, shall we go back to my office and talk about this?"

Once again he charged off, leaving us no chance to refuse. Back in his office he babbled on about the theft, telling us in spite of the intense police investigation nothing definite was ever proved. "One of our employees vanished that same day, and it seems certain he must have been involved."

"Vanished?" Finn asked.

"Yes, our Registrar, Arlie Pott. He had access to all the exhibition pieces. The replica you just saw is used to replace the original when it's loaned out. We might not have known for months that the real Maya head was gone if I hadn't received a request for information on the Ahau glyph on the forehead."

"You've lost me," I said.

"Your own University of Massachusetts is running a field school here. The director of the course has been in contact with me on a regular basis by web cam. He had asked about the sun glyph, the symbol, and I went to fetch the replica to better explain my answer. When I couldn't find it, I had the guards open the case and we discovered the substitution."

"And Mr. Pott…?" Finn asked.

"A good man, or so I thought. He'd been with the museum for twenty-four years."

"Any past history of problems?"

"None at all. That's why it's so puzzling."

"Hmm. Twenty four years is long enough to become dissatisfied with earning a small wage while you're handling artifacts worth millions."

"Then can we count on your help?" the Director again pleaded.

"My focus is still on Aubrey Poulsen, but if I find any connection to the Maya carving I will, of course, pursue it."

That was enough to earn the Director's gratitude and promises of every assistance, and with that we left.

Thirteen

Back at the hotel we found Michael in a state of some excitement. "Bert and Dixie really came through. Take a look at this!"

He waved a sheaf of printouts in front of us. Finn scanned through them; me hanging over his shoulder.

I was shocked. "This certainly changes the perspective, I'd say. What about you, Finn?"

"I'd say it's time we put all this information together and figure out what happened. One of you call down to the hotel desk and ask if we can get a whiteboard up here."

For the next several hours Finn sifted through everything we had, making notes on the board then crossing them out, drawing connecting lines between fragments of information, circling phrases and underscoring. Michael and I stared at the board but saw only a jumble of words.

At one point my phone rang. It was Doren, "Just checking in," he said, "to see how Finn is doing and if you've made any progress."

I mouthed "Doren" to Finn and he gave a slight shake of his head. "He's resting," I lied, "and there's nothing new so far."

We made desultory conversation before I ended with, "Thanks for calling. I'll let you know if anything new turns up," then turned my attention to Finn.

He was staring into space, stroking his beard the way he does when deep in thought.

"Finn?"

He didn't move.

"Finn," I shook him gently, "perhaps you should take a break. Why don't we go down to the tavern? We can sit on the deck and get some fresh air and have a bite to eat. You'll think more clearly afterwards."

"You're right." He pinched the bridge of his nose. "I'm getting a bit of a headache anyway. But first I need to talk to Inspector Usher."

"Can't it wait?"

"It's imperative that I get hold of him right away. One of you see if you can get him on the phone."

Michael jumped into action.

"And tell him it's about the jade carving," Finn added. *What on earth…?*

A while later we headed downstairs. I'd listened in astonishment to Finn's discussion with the inspector. When he'd hung up he turned to me and Michael, "Well, there's nothing now but to wait."

So we found ourselves a shady spot at the tavern overlooking the sea and shared calamari and nachos while Finn told stories of diving with Sir Arthur C. Clarke.

"*The* Arthur C. Clarke," Michael was astonished, "who wrote *2001: A Space Odyssey*?"

"The same," Finn said.

"I didn't know he was a diver."

"People think of him as a futurist, inventor and science fiction writer, but he was also an avid scuba diver and undersea explorer. He discovered the wreck of an Indian treasure ship belonging to the Mughal Emperor, Aurangzeb. He was a great man."

We hung out until after the sun had set. There was still no word from Usher so we called it a night. Though he wouldn't admit to being tired, Finn looked drawn. It had been a really long day and I figured we could all do with a good night's sleep. So we headed for our respective rooms, agreeing to meet at breakfast in the morning.

Fourteen

I was staring down Mick Jagger's tonsils. He kept telling me "You can't always get what you want," but in my half-awake state I definitely didn't want to hear what he had to say, so I pulled the sheet up over my head. Mick just wouldn't shut up, though, and with a start I realized I was actually listening to my cell phone ringing. My hand snaked out to grab the phone – too late. It stopped. Rubbing the sleep from my eyes I looked at the call record – Finn. Then I noticed the time – six.

I stabbed redial. The second he answered I blurted out, "What's wrong?"

"Nothing's wrong."

"Why are you calling me this early if nothing's wrong?"

"I got an answer from Usher. I know what happened."

It had been agreed that we hold a meeting in the hotel. On Finn's behalf I'd called Russell Longsworth and Doren Gillett. When they arrived we arranged ourselves in Finn's suite.

"Did you find out something about Aubrey?" Gillett asked.

"Do you know where the jade head is?" Longsworth wanted to know.

"All in good time," Finn said. "We're waiting for one more person."

Minutes later when there was a knock on the door I opened it to let Inspector Antoine Usher in. He acknowledged Finn with a nod of his head then moved to the side of the room where he stood, hands behind his back.

Finn stepped in front of us.

"You're here because you have an interest in the disappearance of Aubrey Poulsen or the theft of the Maya jade carving. *My* interest, initially, was just in Aubrey. As for the theft of the jade, I looked upon that only as something that detracted from the official investigation into Aubrey's disappearance. But so many other people assumed that I was here to find the jade that I began to wonder if, perhaps, the two incidents *were* connected. The little girl vanished on the same day as the jade. Was that more than coincidence?

"Let me tell you what else we know about both cases.

"First, we were told by Pipaluk Poulsen that she and husband, Lenard, lost their daughter on Ambergris Caye during the San Pedro Festival. The police are notified but they're consumed with the theft of the country's greatest national treasure, a Maya jade carving. So the Poulsens hire a private detective to conduct a search." Here Finn gestured toward Gillett.

"Gillett is very thorough in his search. He can afford to be. He already knows Aubrey Poulson is dead."

"What the hell are you saying?" Gillett shot to his feet, fists clenched, shoulders bunched.

At the same time Usher opened the door and two armed police officers entered to stand sentinel on either side.

"Sit down," the inspector demanded.

Slowly Gillett sank back into his seat, his body taut, his expression wary.

"Alrighty then," said Finn. "I'll go on.

"At the water taxi docks in Belize City, Aubrey is seen on the morning of her disappearance. An eye witness later sees her with a woman getting off the water taxi at Caye Caulker and on to a private boat nearby. Nobody, not the police, not a resident, not a worker, sees the child arrive in San Pedro or anywhere else on Ambergris Caye. So it is somewhere between the two islands that Aubrey disappears.

"Now, on the same day there's yet another disappearance. Coincidence? I don't think so. Arlie Pott, who is Registrar at the Belize Museum, has taken the day off to attend the San Pedro festival, or so he has said. It is purely by chance the theft of the Maya head is discovered that day. As for Mr. Pott, he is never seen or heard of again.

"Several months after Aubrey vanishes, Lenard Pipaluk dies, quite possibly suicide. Reports are that he had begun to drink heavily and his wife said they were broke. I began to wonder why a man who truly loves his child would kill himself. Surely, if there's even the slightest chance Aubrey is alive, Lenard would do everything in his power to keep looking for her. Or did Lenard already know what had happened?

"Something else bothered me. How were the Poulsens able to afford a vacation in Belize when, supposedly, they had very little money? So, with the help of Detective Dixie Tanner back in Florida and a couple other people, I did some digging. Turns out, both Lenard and his wife had rap sheets as long as your arm; lots of petty theft, a few domestic violence calls and Lenard had done a couple of years in prison as the driver in a heist gone wrong. Here's the really interesting part – he was driving a boat."

Finn paused for effect, then cleared his throat and continued.

"There's more. Neither Lenard nor Luki had a job, yet they suddenly had money for plane tickets and a hotel room in Belize. Who gave it to them, and why?

"That's where you come in, Doren."

The private eye began to rise from his chair again but Usher had moved behind him and shoved him back down, keeping a strong hand on his shoulder.

Gillett sputtered. "This is completely absurd. Whatever you're trying to accuse me of doing, it won't fly. I spent months, and I spent my own money, searching for Aubrey. Why would I do that if I didn't believe she was alive? And if you think I had anything to do with the Maya head being stolen, you're crazy. And what about the thugs who kidnapped you? They're probably the ones who took it in the first place. What about that, then?"

Gillett's voice had gone up an octave during his tirade but the only sign it had affected Finn was a slight tightening of the mouth and narrowing of the eyes. And when Finn spoke again his voice had a hard edge.

"I'll tell you exactly what I'm accusing you of, Gillett. You are the one who planned the theft of the jade head. Somehow you persuaded Arlie Pott to switch the real artifact with the replica and carry it from the museum into the care of the Poulsens."

Gillett snorted in derision but Finn ignored him.

"You hired the Poulsens to get the jade out to San Pedro where it was to be handed off to you under cover of the festival. After all, who would pay attention to another family of tourists? Pott had already told people he was going to the festival so, to be true to his story, he also had to get on the taxi. Here's where things started to go wrong. The theft was discovered and suddenly the police were everywhere.

"But you'd planned for that possibility, hadn't you? You had a boat at Caye Caulker. I'm guessing the back-up plan was to hide the jade on Hicks Caye or Caye Chapel and come back for it when the heat died down. There was a problem, though. Arlie Pott panicked when he realized his duplicity was uncovered. Not surprising, really. I don't suppose many museum registrars are cut out to be hardened criminals. He was supposed to stay on the taxi all the way to San Pedro but he followed the Poulsens on to the other boat."

"You're making all this up," the PI sneered.

Finn shook his head. "We know you arranged for the boat, Gillett. Once we knew the Poulsens had picked up a boat on Caye Caulker it didn't take Inspector Usher's men long to find out whose boat it was. By the way, it's never a good idea to use a drunk to transact business for you. Your guy tried to cheat the boat owner and he was able to give a very vivid description of him to the police."

A light sheen of sweat appeared on Gillett's upper lip. At last his nerve was beginning to crack.

"What happened on the boat, Gillett? Was there a fight? How did Aubrey die? We're going to find out anyway. The police in Austin, Texas picked up Luki Poulsen about an hour ago. They're questioning her now."

"You have nothing on me."

"We know you lived in Austin before you went to Oxford. I'm betting you knew the Poulsens then. How long do you think it will take before Luki admits it?"

This time Gillett shrugged away from Usher's grip and stood. "I'm leaving."

Usher nodded at his officers who promptly blocked the doorway. At the same time the inspector grabbed Gillett's arm and twisted it behind his back. But Gillett wasn't having any of that. He kicked back hard, just missing Usher's groin though still able to cause some serious hurt, and the inspector lost his grip and doubled over. Gillett lunged in the direction of the door as Michael,

Finn and both officers threw themselves at him. The PI was really strong and more than a little motivated. He tossed the men aside and got his hand on the door handle, which is when I smashed him over the head with a lamp and he went down like a light. *I can be really funny sometimes.*

Doren Gillett was defeated. Slumped over he sat on the corner of the bed, his hands cuffed behind him and one leg cuffed to a leg of the bed. Usher was nursing a bruised thigh and a bruised ego. The other guys had various minor scrapes and bruises; I was feeling pretty damn good.

"But where's the jade head?"

We all turned to look at Russell Longsworth. I'd practically forgotten about him, he'd been so quiet.

"Yeah, where is the jade head?" I echoed. This time we all turned to Gillett. He raised his head slowly.

"It's in the Caribbean Sea."

We waited. Gillett sighed and continued.

"Arlie Pott was really scared and wanted to try and slip the jade head back into the museum and pretend it had never been stolen. Lenard was driving and Arlie was begging him to change course but Lenard refused. So Arlie grabbed the jade head and threatened to throw it overboard if he didn't. They grappled and somehow Lenard got hold of the jade. According to Luki he swung round with it in his fist as he snatched it away. What he didn't know was that Aubrey was right behind him. He hit her in the head with enough momentum to smash her skull open. She was dead almost instantly.

"They were all horrified. No-one was steering the boat and no-one was paying attention to where it was going. Lenard still had the Maya head in his hand. Whether in anger or grief or shock, he hurled it away. Arlie threw himself after it but slipped, fell hard and broke his neck."

Dear Lord. The story was the worse for Gillett's emotionless telling of it.

"Lenard cracked. Luki managed to stop the boat and drop anchor. They had to get rid of the bodies but Lenard wouldn't let go of his daughter and was freaking out about dropping her in the water. It took Luki a couple of hours to persuade Lenard to release his hold but he was still useless; just sat and sobbed. Luki had to do everything alone. She knew she had to weight the bodies and she must have done a decent job of it except for that foot breaking loose."

He looked directly at Finn and gave a hollow laugh. "Of all the shitty luck, it gets swept into the Gulf of Mexico where you have to find it."

Softly Finn responded, "You're finally getting the luck you really deserve."

"I don't understand why Luki Poulsen told Michael about Doren Gillett in the first place. If she'd just said the police investigated her daughter's disappearance but nothing was found, she might have stopped our search before it began."

"She couldn't be sure of that," Finn answered. "If we'd later found out about Gillett we'd wonder why she hadn't told us about him. She'd start to look pretty suspicious. And the art of getting away with a con is to stick as closely to the truth as possible."

"So that's why Gillett continued to act as a private detective."

"That, and he needed a reason to stick around so he could search for the Maya head. People knew him as an avid recreational diver when his only interest was finding the jade."

I picked up my glass and took a sip. "Mmm. This really is good."

We were sitting at the Tavern bar in the Radisson waiting for our taxi to the airport. All the talk of Maya artifacts had inspired me to think up a "Maya Cocktail." With the bartender's help I'd infused a little chili pepper in cinnamon vodka and combined it with chocolate liqueur and a touch of vanilla. Add a lime garnish and we were good to go.

By the way, if any of you are curious about the use of Maya and Mayan, the simple rule of thumb is that Mayan is only used in reference to the language. "Maya" is both a noun and an adjective, so… Maya people, Maya artifact, Maya food and on. Now you can go and impress someone.

Fifteen

Joshua Bumbry stood between his parents, hugging the memorial wreath to him as Finn spoke his final words:

Although this dear young child
Was with us just a while
She'll live on in our hearts
With a sweet remembered smile

Time Voyager's engines were silent as she lay at anchor where it had all begun with the finding of a little girl's pink sneaker. Joshua looked up at his mother; she put her hand on his back, gently urging him to the boat's side. With both arms he threw the wreath across the water. It landed with barely a splash and for a long time we all watched as it bobbed slowly along. Then a ripple of disturbance caught our attention and we gasped as a pair of bottlenose dolphins leapt high in the air on either side of the wreath. Once, twice, three times they dazzled us.

Joshua's mood changed instantly from somber to joyous. He pumped the air with his fist, "Hooray for Aubrey," then burst into laughter. Soon we were laughing with him.

"What an amazing tribute," Grace Bumbry said.

"And see, Mom, it was a good thing we got the bio-degradable wreath."

"I'm very proud of you for thinking of it," his mother smiled down at him.

We stayed on the site until the wreath disappeared over the horizon, then upped anchor and made way for Sarasota.

A little while later I found Joshua curled up on the sofa with Shrimp. He had his serious face on again. "You OK, buddy?"

His lip quivered a little. "Do you believe in Heaven?"

I sat beside him. "What's all this about?"

"I want to believe Aubrey went to Heaven, but it's not like going to a house or, or school, or maybe even a boat. You can't see it, so how do you know it's there?"

"Hmm." I thought for a moment. "Remember how we watched the wreath 'til it disappeared?" He nodded. "Just because we couldn't see it any more, does that mean it doesn't exist?"

"Of course not. It's just out of sight. Oh!" He clapped his hands. "I get it. We can't see my house right now but I know it's there."

"And you can't see your school, but you know it will be there when you have to go back on Monday." He grimaced a little at that. "Sorry," I added.

"It's OK. You're the best."

"No, you're the best," and I hugged him, squishing Shrimp between us, but she didn't seem to mind.

Sixteen

It was day fifteen of the search for the jade Maya Head. At the urging of Russell Longsworth the Belizean government had requested Finn's assistance in recovery efforts. Conjecture based on Luki Poulsen's account of events put the sculpture somewhere south and west of Ambergris Caye, and north of Caye Caulker. That still covered a hell of a lot of water. The good news was it put the artifact on the shallow shelf that runs from the shoreline to the barrier reef. On the east side of the reef the waters progressively approach thirteen thousand feet: that would have killed any chance of finding the jade. As it was, we were working at about sixty feet.

Finn was ready to take a turn to go down. We'd tried side scan sonar initially, which creates an image of the sea floor as it's towed behind the boat. Problem was, there were so many wrecks on the ocean floor and so much scatter – dispersal from the wrecks – it was impossible to detect one piece of jade. So Finn opted to do things the old-fashioned way and do circular searches.

Because sixty feet is the level at which you have to start worrying about decompression, Finn was adhering to the 60/60 rule of thumb: at sixty feet, you could only stay under for sixty minutes. He had a team of six divers, including himself. Each day, four of them would rotate one hour underwater, diving three times, with three hours to decompress between dives. The other two would sit out.

After Finn's kidnap scare I'd been a bit reluctant to return to Belize, but you just can't keep a good shipwreck treasure hunter above water. As it turned out, the thugs were soon apprehended. They were one of all too many gangs who'd heard the same misleading chatter about us looking for the Maya sculpture. I was still concerned, but it helped to be surrounded each day by a group of testosterone-loaded men. *Who am I kidding? It was great.* It soothed my ego as well. I'd thought Doren Gillett actually liked me, but he'd only been sticking close to keep track of our investigation and try and steer us the wrong way.

The most recent diver had surfaced and he gave Finn the GPS coordinates for where he'd left off the search. Finn took a large step forward and into the water. He gave the OK signal and disappeared. Several other people were keeping watch so I retreated to the shade for a little shut-eye. I was just in that state of before and after when I heard a shout. "Hey!" *Finn.*

I bounded to port and rested my hands on the gunwale. "Are you OK?"

"Yes. I'm coming aboard."

He swam to the boat where several pairs of hands pulled him up. His mesh bag looked suspiciously heavy.

"Don't tell me…" I said.

"OK, I won't."

By now the others had crowded around and were urging him to disclose his find. He pulled an object from the bag and, with a flourish, lifted it skyward.

The Maya head.

There were cheers and back-clapping and general euphoria.

"I knew you would do it," I grinned.

We were heading back to the dock where Russell Longsworth was to greet us. Finn and I were watching the salvage site recede.

"There's a Spanish wreck down there," Finn said.

Startled, I turned my head to him. "Are you sure?"

"I saw the outline of a cannon, and some other scatter."

"Do you think the government will give us a salvage permit?"

"I doubt it, but it's worth a try. Maybe they'll feel like rewarding us for finding their national treasure."

As it was, the Belizean government expressed their eternal gratitude to us, but they weren't sufficiently grateful to allow us to recover any other wreckage. Amazing, isn't it? We spend months, sometimes years, carefully searching for shipwreck history without success. When we find something by accident we're not allowed to touch it.

The End

The next book is:
The Boneyard Murder

Become part of the in-crowd and get a FREE short story:
http://lizdodwell.com/signup/

Find all of Liz's books here:
http://lizdodwell.com/books/

Author's Notes

Well, here we are again. Captain Finn has solved his fourth mystery.

You should know there really is a sculpture of the Maya Sun God, Kinich Ahau at the Museum of Belize. It was thought by many to have been stolen shortly after its discovery though is, in fact, safely under lock and key. None-the-less, it was my inspiration for this treasure tale.

Although "The Game's A Foot" is a work of fiction, I do try very hard to be factual in much of the detail and I hope you appreciate that authenticity. If you ever read anything that is glaringly wrong, please do let me know. You can always reach me on my facebook page: facebook.com/LizDodwellAuthor. And, hey, go ahead and give me your thoughts anyway. Maybe you have a great idea for a new treasure mystery. I'd love to hear it.

Once again I need to send out a big thank you to Carl Fismer, shipwreck treasure hunter and friend of the first order. He puts up with my phone calls requesting clarification on all kinds of stuff and is an absolute mine of information. Why not check him out at CarlFismer.com?

And, always, thanks to my husband, Alex, who is a rock. Most of all, thank you, my wonderful readers. You're the reason I do this.

The Boneyard Murder

"Are there killer whales in the Gulf of Mexico?"

Finn gave me a look that said, *Now what?* But the words he voiced were, "Some have been spotted in deep water."

"But not where we are now?"

"No."

"Then what's that swimming over there?"

His eyes followed the direction of my pointing arm, then narrowed and two creases appeared between his brows.

"Jafet," he called out to our diver who was driving the boat, "toss me those binos."

Jafet pulled the binoculars from their perch and threw them to Finn. For some minutes he gazed across the water.

"Turn ten degrees to port," Finn directed, "and keep it slow and steady."

"What is it?" I was on tenterhooks, snatching the binos from Finn's grasp. It took me a few moments to focus them. "Oh my god. It's a dog!"

As we got closer I began calling to the pooch, "Here boy, come on. Good puppy, you can do it." Either he didn't hear or it didn't register.

"He's probably in shock," Finn said. Still I kept up a constant jabber of encouragement.

"Get the inflatable ready," Finn said. "I don't want to get too close with *Time Voyager*."

My eyes were riveted on the dog and I was about to jump to Finn's bidding when I realized the animal's hindquarters were beginning to sink. I saw his front legs lift out of the water in frantic motion and his head pull back to keep his nose up. "Too late, he's in trouble," I yelled and in the next instant was over the side.

There was a slight chop on the water but I powered towards the struggling hound. I heard Finn's voice, "Come up behind him. He might panic and try to bite."

I did just that; put an arm around him as he was about to go under. His body instantly went slack and I quickly rolled on to my back, pulling him on top of me. By now Finn and Enos – our second diver - had the inflatable in the water and were heading my way, which was a good thing because the dog was a dead weight and I was struggling to keep his head out of the water.

Soon, hands reached out and plucked the dog from my chest and hauled me into the inflatable with him. I pulled myself into a crouch; the half dead beast just lay there.

"Is he breathing?" I asked.

For answer, Finn held the dog upside down and I watched water drip from his nose and mouth. As Enos zipped us back to the boat Finn lay the dog on its side and pressed his fingertips gently on the back of one of the front paws.

94

"There's a faint heartbeat." Then he lay his hand on the animal's chest to feel for movement and placed his cheek next to its nose. "He doesn't seem to be breathing."

By now we were at the boat. Finn carried the dog into the salon, laying him on the sofa. He pulled the mutt's tongue forward so it wouldn't form an obstruction then, holding the mouth closed he blew into the snout. He did this several times before taking a break to see if the dog would breathe on its own. Nothing; so he repeated the exercise. This time when he stopped we watched the dog's chest continue to rise.

"You did it!" I clapped Finn on the back. "You're brilliant. What should we do now?"

"Get him dried off and then wrap him in a blanket. We need to keep him warm or he might go into shock."

In an earlier part of his life Finn had been a paramedic, so it was no surprise he knew what to do to save a dog's life. He's also a big softie and would do everything he could to help a creature in need. Anyway, I hurried to gather up the supplies and as I re-entered the salon Jafet stepped in beside me.

"I came to meet the new guest," he said.

Jafet Quintana and Enos Donnell were best friends who worked with us from time to time. Both competent divers, they were also experienced boatmen and between them could fix just about anything. When they weren't on *Time Voyager* they worked for themselves doing a variety of construction jobs.

Jafet looked past me to the sofa and a startled look crossed his face. "I know that dog."

In unison Finn and I turned his way.

"He belongs to a couple who have a booth at the Red Barn."

We nodded in understanding. Jafet's wife, Elodia, sold homemade candles every weekend at the Red Barn flea market in Bradenton, just north of Sarasota. It's an enormous place but Elodia had been set up there for years and knew many of the vendors.

"Who are they?" Finn asked.

"Umm, Mark is his name, I'm pretty sure. His wife is Katy...Kaylee...something like that. I do know they both dive. I've talked to them a couple of times when I've been there to help Elodia pack up."

"Any chance they could have been out diving today?" Finn's voice had an edge to it.

"You mean the dog could have fallen overboard?"

"That's one possibility."

Get the next book here:

The Boneyard Murder

Become part of the in-crowd and get a FREE short story:

http://lizdodwell.com/signup/

Find all of Liz's books here:

http://lizdodwell.com/books/

Liz Dodwell

…was told so many times that she really knew how to spin a yarn, she finally decided to put that talent to good use. Taking inspiration from her good friend and real-life treasure hunter, Captain Carl Fismer, she created the Captain Finn Treasure Mystery series.

For several years Liz worked with the Captain, operating his website and arranging talks and treasure exhibitions. "I would dive when I got the chance, but only on a hookah," she says. "I never found anything of real importance, but just knowing I was getting even a microscopic glimpse of history and adventure was truly exciting."

Fueled by an occasional cup of grog, Liz writes from the home she shares with husband Alex and a crew of rescued dogs and cats. For a change of pace she pens stories in cozy mystery and romantic suspense. For relaxation she likes to yodel. (Just kidding).

www.LizDodwell.com